Copyri

First electrc

All rights are reserv
be used or reproduce... any manner whatsoever
without written permission, except in the case of brief
quotations embodied in critical articles and reviews.
The unauthorised reproduction or distribution
of this copyrighted work is illegal. No part of this
book may be scanned, uploaded, or distributed
via the internet or any other means, electronic or
print, without the author's express permission.

Note from the Author:
This book is a work of fiction. The names, characters,
and incidents are products of the writer's imagination
or have been used fictitiously and are not to be
construed as real. Any resemblance to persons,
living or dead, actual events, or organisations is
entirely coincidental. The author does not have any
control over and does not assume any responsibility
for third-party websites or their content.

Published in the United Kingdom.
Cover Design: Red Light Book Covers

This book is written in British English. This means that there will be additional letters in words (i.e. colour instead of color), words will end in '-ised' instead of '-ized', and '-tre' instead of '-ter'.

Dedication:

For all those who have suffered shitty Valentine's Days, I hope this makes you laugh.

For the 'heroes/heroines' out there doing the hard yards on the Hub and OF, thank you for your inspiration.

∞∞∞

And lastly, for Charlene Kilgore Kiney. You raised a fantastic daughter, and I think you would've got a kick out of this one.

Chapter One

"Jane! Jane? Where are you, Jane?"

I looked up as my flat-mate Lucille barged through my bedroom door, her normally coiffed and elegant honey-blonde tresses dishevelled. Excitement and a dash of anxiety brightened her azure eyes. Her porcelain skin was flushed, bringing an unnatural pink stain to her high cheekbones.

"Luce, what's the matter? Are you alright?"

"Oh, Jane, you'll never guess what's happened!" Lucille waved something in my face, white and crinkling with each movement. It was an envelope, that much I could tell, but I couldn't read any of the fine details. Not with how buzzed she was.

"Luce, calm down! Do you want me to play 'guess the news', or will you simply tell me what's got you in such a tizzy? For Lucifer's sake, you're in a right state!"

Lucille nodded and took a deep breath to settle her nerves. I loved my flat-mate, it was impossible not to. Succubi like us don't just feed and prey on sexual deviances and lust. We also inspire love, promote fertility, and get the biggest kick when we can play matchmaker. That first crush? Then the flush of new love which deepens to true desire, nurturing it into producing new life? That can sustain a succubus easily without draining the life of the source. Strip clubs, sex clubs, and prostitution can gorge us short-term, but the underlying need for more will never be satisfied, not like when feeding from a loving relationship.

My dithering allowed Lucille to quieten down, to tuck her hair behind her ears, smooth down her short skirt, and to allow her heaving bosoms to stop, well, heaving.

"Oh, Jane! A courier just dropped this off, it's from the Ministry of Earthly Desires. I think these are our orders!"

I reached out with a trembling hand. Could it be? Was it really our turn? Lucille passed me the thick envelope and I saw the official stamp at the top left corner. Yes, it was from the Ministry alright and addressed to both Lucille and I. I looked up into my fellow succubi's eyes and she nodded to go ahead. I tore open the envelope, fumbling the contents out and onto my bed, where minutes ago, I'd been resting.

A cover letter lay on top and I picked it up, scanning it before I read aloud:

Attn: Ms. Lucille Luxure & Ms. Jane Chérir
The Ministry of Earthly Desires have processed your applications for relocation to Earth. Congratulations. Your requests have been approved and your assigned postings are contained within this packet.

MY VALENTINE'S SUCKS!(UBUS)

You have one Hell month from the date of this correspondence to research your new home and prospective careers. You will be issued with a 12-Earth month probationary period, after which you may choose to either stay on Earth for your remaining tenure, or return to Hell. If you choose to return, you may not reapply for reassignment for a minimum of 10 Hell years.

As this is your first appointment, the duration of your tenure will be 50 Earth years, including the probationary period. Please prepare appropriately, include a minimum of three aliases, and have the relevant ageing glamours and fashions for each identity.

My voice tapered off as I looked up to where Lucille sat at my dresser, visibly vibrating with excitement.

"We're going? We're really going?" I whispered, my voice hoarse.

"We're going! We're really going!" Lucille squealed, her voice suffused with glee.

Well shit. It looked like I was about to take my very first trip to Earth.

∞∞∞

It had been a tumultuous month. Both Lucille and I had delved deeply into the Hub, where the majority of our modern research regarding current life on Earth was held. Our libraries were full of manuscripts, text books, and individual journals and recounts. It also included the more popular fiction texts, although some were closer to being more factual. It was amusing to see how many variations of Mothman there were, generally based on when Princes Dis, Azazel, or Astaroth had been sighted in the area. King Belphegor himself was quite pleased with how humans thought him a wendigo whenever he visited.

I loved learning. I was considered as quite young for a succubus, only 27 in Hell years. Although that equated to much older in Earth years. Ever since I'd learned to read I'd devoured information on Earth and found several Earthly occupations fascinating. Before receiving permission to travel to Earth, I had gained knowledge equivalent to doctorates in several degrees as well as multiple trades. I wanted to make the most of my time there, so I researched several different career paths via the Hub.

I'd lined up my first job as a paediatric nurse, and had my uniform prepared for my first day. I also had several others as backup, one for each alternate career. The Ministry had organised my accommodation. All that was left was to finish packing and make my way to the Portal. I was a bit sad that I wouldn't have Lucille with me, but she was headed to a completely different continent. She was heading to Las Vegas, Nevada to be a showgirl, as she'd always to wanted to visit and loved performing. Me though? I was heading to London, England. Or at least one of the cities nearby.

"Oh my Lucifer, I'm going to miss you girl! Are you sure I can't change your mind? Las Vegas has nurses too, you know?"

Lucille wrapped her slender arms around me and pulled me tight into her embrace. She'd prepared well for her new post and had inflated her already-generous boobs to an even more prominent cup size. I pulled away from her, bussed her cheek with a quick kiss, and squeezed her hands.

"Yes Luce, I'm sure. I want to try something different. If it doesn't work out, then maybe I can come over and join you. But for my first year at least, I want to try and stick it out there. Besides just think of it, I could end up nursing Tom Hiddleston back to health!"

We'd both lusted over him in the movie 'High Rise', but we adored him as Loki, full of mischief and cheek.

Lucille giggled then pressed her own plush lips to my cheek.

"I'm gonna miss you sweetheart. You've got my number though, yeah?"

I nodded and patted the device issued to me by the Ministry. It was amazing. A camera, phone, computer, and e-reader in one. So much human ingenuity is credited to them selling their souls, but that's a complete fallacy. A fairy-tale humans tell their children to scare them into conformity.

Lucille wandered out of my room and over to her own as I closed the lid of my suitcase, tugged the zippers together then extended the handle to wheel it out. Our flat was empty of our belongings, packed away and sent to our joint storage unit for the duration of our times on Earth. I took one last look at the place I'd called home for the last nine Hell years and then trailed Lucille out the door. The snick of the lock behind us echoed through the empty hall and reflected the end of this chapter of my life. Now was the time for a new beginning, and I was excited to get started.

Chapter Two

Croydon...wasn't what I expected. I walked out of the shadows of the East Croydon train station, my suitcase bumping noisily behind me, and blinked at the sensory overload. Noise—the rumble of trains passing below my feet, the hubbub of multiple conversations, cars honking and revving their engines. Smells—the fumes of hot exhaust, unwashed bodies, and rotting garbage. People bumped and jostled me in their rush to catch their train, not to mention the weather. I'd heard England was a very wet country, but thought it a joke. It was summer, it was supposed to be sunny and warm, not overcast and miserable!

I was lucky my new flat was close to the station as I had no umbrella to keep me dry, and the rain, while not heavy, was constant. I pulled up the map app on my device, plugged in the address and within minutes I was dripping my way across the foyer of my apartment building. I made my way across a warm blonde tiled floor, the heels of my shoes clacking loudly. Their short, sharp raps echoed like gunshots in the quiet. The concierge desk was manned by an attractive woman, her ash-blonde hair styled and cut in a neat bob that tucked along her jawline. Her attention currently sat on the ginger-haired man stood at the other side of her desk. A professional yet friendly smile sat on her cherry-coated lips, and her nails were neat and manicured as they slid him a pamphlet. I slowed my steps as I approached. When he turned away, I caught sight of dark framed glasses, a strong jaw, and freckles. I watched as he walked away, oblivious to my attention. His slender frame was covered in a loose linen shirt tucked in at one side, with tailored trousers hugging his tight arse and thighs in all the right places. I sighed, appreciating the view as he disappeared around a corner, when a small hint of lust hit my nostrils. I turned back to the concierge and her eyes met mine with a sparkle.

"One thing I love about working here is the amazing views I'm treated to every day. Oh, don't worry," she laughed at me, mischief sparkling in her eyes as she waved a finger in my direction, the glitter of a diamond band catching my eye, "I'm happily married, but there's no harm in looking. Especially not when my husband appreciates the end results." She chuckled once more before donning a more professional and detached persona.

"Hello, and welcome to Whitestar Apartments. My name is Liz. How may I be of assistance today?"

I smiled back and extended one hand. Glancing down at it she took it in her own as I introduced myself.

"Hello, I'm Jane Chérir, and I'm a new tenant

here. My agent, M.E.D. Inc., arranged everything for me."

After giving my hand a firm shake, Liz dropped it to tap away at the computer tucked away to one side of her desk.

"Ah yes, Ms. Chérir, I have you right here. A one bedroom apartment, for twelve months. You're on the 23rd floor, in number five." She handed me a key, a decorative starburst fob dangling from it with the number 2305 discreetly hidden in the central scrollwork. I had to bite back a chuckle at the number. Someone back in Hell had a sense of humour because both the numbers of my apartment and the floor it sat on were considered evil or unholy in some circles. After a few more minutes, Liz handed me a welcome packet and gestured toward a set of lifts which whisked me up to the 23rd floor with quiet efficiency.

I stepped out from between the open doors, my steps loud on the parquetry. Noting the signage that directed me to my apartment, I turned the corner and then stopped. Standing in the hallway was the ginger-haired man. My heart gave a little flutter when he looked up toward me. His gaze speared into mine. The green of his eyes was almost a smoky blue in the dim lighting, the scruff of his beard not hiding the shallow cleft of his chin in the slightest. His glasses, those thick black frames, had slid down his nose slightly and his hair tumbled over his forehead in tousled curls. I could see his body outlined through his shirt, long and lean with the sleeves rolled up to show strong forearms. The view of his front was just as appealing as his rear. My eyes travelled back up to his face to catch him eyeing me in return. His skin blushed an adorable shade of red the moment he realised I'd caught him checking me out. I smiled to soften the embarrassment.

"Hello, I'm Jane, and I believe I'm your new neighbour." I introduced myself as I glanced at his door number, noting he was in number four, and my door was just beyond where he stood. He cleared his throat and blushed again, then quirked a self-deprecating half-smile at me.

"Uh, hi, I'm Jamie. Jamie Coffey. Sorry 'bout staring, you just startled me is all. You're the first to move onto this floor besides me." He reached out with his hand, and I accepted, shaking it firmly. We stood there for a moment, the silence descending toward the awkward, until I gestured past him to my own door.

"Well Jamie, it was lovely to meet you. I'm going to get myself settled, so I'll see you around?" Why did I end that on a question? I felt a bit flustered, but then again, Jamie was only the second human I'd spoken to so far.

"Uh, yeah, sure. See you 'round." And then he was gone, softly closing his door behind him. Mentally giving myself a shake, I headed toward the last door in the hallway, the brass number '5' gleaming in the light. Home sweet home. At least for the next twelve months.

Chapter Three

Excitement trilled its way through my body. Today was the first day of my new job. I had my bag all ready to go with my uniform stowed and my lunch packed. I was spoiled for choice here, with several large hospitals within a reasonable bus or train commute. Not to mention the smaller health and medical centres dotted around. I was headed for the University Hospital, which was open 24 hours. I pulled on a pair of capri shorts and a loose tee, a funny slogan about an 'Emotional Support Orc' painted across it, and laced up my brand new trainers.

As I left my apartment, I heard another door shut and looked up to see Jamie locking his own door.

"Heading out, Jane?"

"Yes, I am! I start my new job today, and I'm very excited!"

Jamie smiled that crooked grin of his, then gestured for me to pass by.

"I'm heading out too, I've got to see a man about a dog. Mind if I join you in the lift?"

Laughing at his attempt at gallantry, I shook my head as I walked past. Mmm, he smelled good, and not just because of his cologne. As we waited for the lift to arrive on our floor, we made some small talk, feeling our way toward a tentative friendship.

"Are you really seeing a man about a dog, or were you just using that as an expression?" I asked him, curious. I'd read the information packet Liz had given me my first night here on Earth, and Whitestar Apartments actively encouraged its residents to keep pets, with a pet spa and grooming services on-site. If I decided to stay after my probation was up, I might pick up a pet of my own.

"Yeah, I was serious. I'm headed to a local animal shelter today, and hope to come home with a friend."

"Well, good luck with that, I hope you find what you're looking for."

A ding sounded as the lift arrived on our floor, and the doors opened to show another couple already inside. Everyone exchanged nods and friendly smiles, and our conversation moved on to the upcoming resident event. By the time we reached the ground floor, I'd made friends with Cheryl and Rod, who both lived up on the 32nd floor. They had been married for 20 years and had a teenage daughter. The love and contentment pouring from them left me feeling full. We all parted ways outside the building, Cheryl and Rod heading down toward the Whitgift Centre, whereas Jamie and I crossed the road to the bus terminal next to the train station. My bus was pulling in as we arrived, so I waved my farewell, paid my fare, and took an empty seat, unable to withhold the wide smile beaming across my face.

MY VALENTINE'S SUCKS!(UBUS)

∞∞∞

I couldn't believe it! I didn't understand. Everything had been looking so hopeful, so positive! When I'd interviewed for the nursing position, everyone had seemed so excited to have me on board, yet I'd barely stepped onto the ward floor before the unit manager had sprinted toward me, screaming in my face.

"What the hell lady? No, no this is not appropriate or funny. Get back in there, get dressed, and then get out and never come back!"

I didn't understand. I quickly changed back into my street clothes, neatly folded my uniform and tucked it into my bag, before I slunk out the door. The unit manager was there with hospital security and when I stepped into the hallway she held out a hand, stopping me from going any further.

"I want your hospital lanyard and ID. You are not welcome on these premises unless as a patient. I don't know what stunt you were trying to pull, but it's disgraceful, and so are you. Now get out and stay out."

I pulled my hospital lanyard from my bag and handed it over, the unit manager snatching it rudely before abruptly turning and stalking away. The two security guards didn't speak to me, simply pointing toward the emergency stairwell before they escorted me down and outside.

"Best be doing as Nurse Clackson says, and stay away. I don't know what you've done to tick her off, but it must be awful because she's one of the sweetest, understanding, and easy-going nurses on the Paediatric ward." The guard on my left eyed me with suspicion.

"Yeah, what Mike says. Clackson don't blow her top like that without reason. So if you've given her one, best to stay away. Shame though, you're a pretty one. The kids prolly woulda liked you." The guard on my right eyed me with a more cynical look.

I hunched my shoulders and stumbled away, shame and embarrassment overwhelming me. I didn't understand what I'd done wrong and could only hope this wouldn't prevent me from working at one of the other hospitals or medical centres in the area.

∞∞∞

"I don't understand it though Luce, I don't know what I did wrong. They were so happy with my credentials up until I walked out onto the ward this morning. Then it all fell to shit."

I'd arrived back home with my tail tucked between my legs, awash with shame and confusion. Fortunately, I'd avoided interacting with anyone else and had spent the rest of the day applying for positions at the other hospitals in the area. I got lucky and snapped up a job at a nearby private hospital with an immediate start. I'd spent the rest of the day moping until it was late enough to call Lucille and vent.

"Well, the good news is you landed on your feet. You said this unit manager was female? Maybe she was jealous of you. I mean, I'm pretty sure you're smart enough to be a neurosurgeon, but you're happy to settle as a nurse in a children's ward? Yeah, I think she felt threatened by you."

That was Lucille for you. Loving, supportive, and able to soothe the most ruffled of feathers. We chatted some more about our new lives. Her with her show and costume, and the glitz and glamour of Las Vegas show business. Me with my hopes to influence everyday people. The moment I mentioned my neighbour though, Lucille was like a shark scenting blood in the water.

"Oh? There's only the two of you on your floor and you're right next door to each other? So, tell me more. How old is he? Is he single? Straight or gay? Oooh, maybe he's bi! What does he look like?"

I laughed at her questions and answered them to the best of my ability.

"Okay, so he looks to be in his late 20's to early thirties. I think he's single because I've yet to meet or hear a significant other coming or going, but I can't say for certain. I have no idea of his sexual orientation, but I'm hoping he has at least some interest in the opposite sex. As for how he looks?" I paused for a moment, picturing him in my head.

"He's taller than me, but not quite six foot tall. He's five-ten, five-eleven maybe? He's not skinny, but he's not really bulky either. Sleek is the word that comes to mind, sleek and lithe. He looks to be in shape if his forearms, arse, or thighs are anything to go by. He's got ginger curls, longer on the top and shorter on the sides, and generally has a bit of a beard growing. His eyes are green but change colour in different lights, wears a pair of those chunky black hipster-style glasses, and has freckles. He's pretty cute really."

"Oh, you've found yourself your very own ginger? Does he look anything like Harry?"

I laughed.

"No, he's not remotely like that royal, apart from the hair colour. He's also really quite sweet, if a little awkward around me."

We spoke for another few minutes before ending the call. I needed to head to bed, and Luce needed to prepare for her next show.

∞∞∞

I slammed my front door behind me, then let the tears flow. It had happened again! I'd barely taken two steps outside the locker room before the oncologist I was supposed to be working with had grabbed my arm and dragged me back inside, yelling at me.

"Do you think this is supposed to be funny? Is this some sort of joke to you? Well let me tell you, it isn't remotely amusing, not in the slightest! I'll be reporting you to the NHS and the NMC both, and I'll make sure you never get a job in this industry again! Now get out of here!"

Snatching my lanyard and ID, he'd slammed his way out of the locker room, and heard him yelling for security as I'd hurriedly changed back into my street clothes. I kept telling myself that this was only a setback, that I had other job options out there. I was lucky the Ministry had seeded enough money to cover my costs of living for my probationary period. I'd brusquely walked to the stairwell at the end of the hallway, then ran down each flight of stairs, eager to leave this humiliation behind me.

Sliding down my front door, I let the tears stream down my face. I didn't know how long I sat there wallowing, but a soft knock at my door got me to my feet. Wincing at my tear-drenched image in the mirror hanging above my console table, I wiped them from my face. Peeking through the spy-hole, I saw Jamie standing there, so I opened the door, a watery smile on my lips.

"Hi Jamie, what's up?"

The moment he saw my tear-stained face, the smile on his face fell.

"Hey, Jane, what's the matter? Are you okay?"

"It's just work stuff. I think I need a new career.

Never mind, it's not important. What can I do for you today?"

"Ah, um, okay. Well, I thought I heard your door just before, so thought I'd introduce you to my new friends."

"New friends?"

"Um, yeah. Remember how yesterday I was heading off to the animal shelter to see about a dog? I picked up a couple of new friends. I thought, you know, I'd be neighbourly and introduce you to them?"

I smiled at the thought of meeting an affectionate dog, or even a cat.

"Yeah, I'd love that. Just give me five minutes to wash my face, and I'll come over. Thanks for thinking of me, Jamie."

Blushing, Jamie backed away and headed back to his own door.

"Okay then, I'll put the kettle on and we can have a cuppa while you're over. I'll leave the door unlocked, just come in."

Smiling, I shut the door and hurried to my bathroom. As I washed my face, I felt my spirits lift. I may have lost one career opportunity, but it looked as though I'd found a friend.

∞ ∞ ∞

Jamie

I'm such a bloody idiot. Ever since I'd set eyes on Jane a week ago, I couldn't get her out of my head. I'd find myself searching for a glimpse of her every time I left my apartment. I had even moved down to the co-working space closest to the main foyer in the hopes of spotting her while I worked. Working from home had its perks and being able to dictate my own schedule was one of them.

I'd spotted her rushing past and up the stairs to the upper level lifts this morning, so I had quickly packed up and followed. I knew my excuse was pathetic, my fascination turning into an obsession, but I couldn't help it. Jane was so sweet, so lovely, and not just in appearance. Kindness shone from her brown eyes, an almost permanent smile on her plush lips, and her pale skin seemed to glow with compassion. Why then, did I always seem to end up dreaming of her? Of fisting her long dark hair in one hand, the other gripping the gentle swell of her hips as I pounded into her from behind, her perky arse cushioning each thrust of my hips, her perfect tits swaying to the rhythm? Fuck, now I was hard as stone. I heard the snick of my front door and rushed over to my kitchen, hiding my lower body behind the bench top as I puttered around, filling the kettle, pulling mugs from the cupboard as I frantically willed my dick to subside. By the time the kettle was whistling a boil, my dick had deflated, and I turned to where Jane leaned against the breakfast bar. She was beautiful, even though she'd been in tears not even five minutes ago.

"Tea or coffee? And how do you take it?"

"Coffee please, milk with one sugar."

"Just like me." I quickly made two cups, and handed hers over.

"So, who's your new friend? Where are they?"

I smiled and beckoned for her to follow me into my spare room. Tucked away in a corner was a playpen with a fluffy cat bed. A tabby cat and two kittens, one a beautiful tortoiseshell, the other a tabby like its mother, lay curled up together, snoring softly. Jane let out a soft cry and when I looked to her, her eyes shone with adoration.

"Oh, they're beautiful! Are they a mother and her babies?"

"Yeah. I know I originally went to pick out a dog, but when I saw them all I couldn't resist. The rescue had hoped to home them all together, and I couldn't say no. I'm calling the mum 'Mama', unoriginal I know, but she seems to like it. The kittens are a girl and boy. I've named them Meg and Mog. Meg's the tortie, Mog's the tabby."

Seeing the way she melted and gushed about the snoozing cats had me melting inside. Dammit, this girl was a danger to my solitary life, and I didn't give a rat's arse.

Chapter Four

It had taken several weeks to get things sorted after my abrupt exit from nursing, but I'd come to Earth prepared. I'd initially chosen it to help people, so my next choice held the same intention, just with a different method of delivery.

While I'd waited for my applications to go through, I'd come to know Jamie quite well. His family was from 'up north', somewhere up in the Midlands, and he was a freelance web developer. He'd moved to London several years ago for a job, but had quit because he was tired of being overworked, underpaid, and taken advantage of. He'd become a bit of a hermit, so when the opportunity to move into Whitestar Apartments had come up, he'd grabbed it with both hands. He'd found the idea of communal areas and resident events attractive, and the lifestyle arrangements suited him to a tee. He'd been able to form a few friendships since moving in, ours being one of them.

"I'm glad you're my neighbour, Jane. I'm glad we met and you've been willing to get to know me. I'm not the most outgoing of people, so this friendship of ours? It's important to me."

We were inside the lift, on our way downstairs.

I had my bag slung over my shoulder, my uniform pressed and ready, and my hair was braided and tucked away neatly. Jamie had his laptop bag slung over one shoulder, his travel coffee mug in one hand, a baby monitor in the other. He'd discovered the hard way that, if left to their own devices with no supervision, Meg and Mog would reduce soft furnishings to ribbons and scraps over the course of an afternoon. His solution? Install a baby monitor with video capabilities for when he was required to attend virtual meetings and conferences. That way, he could keep an eye on them while he worked but not have to worry about them chewing through his assortment of cables and leads.

"Thanks Jamie. I'm glad we're friends too."'

"Are you nervous about today? New job and all..."

I thought for a moment, but smiled.

"No, I feel really good about this. I'm more than qualified, I want to help people, and they're screaming for new recruits. I think this might be the perfect job for me."

"Well, good luck with holding that thin blue line, PC Chérir, and I'll be sure to keep my nose clean to make your job easier!"

Laughing, we parted ways, Jamie toward the private meeting rooms, and me out the front doors. I was eager to start my life as a Police Constable for the Metropolitan Police Service.

MY VALENTINE'S SUCKS!(UBUS)

∞ ∞ ∞

"Out! Fuck me dead, what the bleedin' hell do you think you're playing at? Fuck off, get out, don't let the door hit you where the good Lord split you!"

Unbelievable! It's happening all over again, and I don't understand it. Everything was going so well, I'd been given a quick tour of the station, and then gone to change into my uniform after clocking in. I'd been about to push open the doors to the main floor when I'd been yanked into an office, where my Sergeant proceeded to harangue me.

"Gordon bloody Bennett, what goes through those thick skulls of kids today? You'd make us a right laughing-stock if you went out in public! We've got a hard enough bloody job without you mucking it up! Go on, get your kit, and piss off!"

I raced back to the locker room, struggled back into my street clothes, stuffed my uniform into the depths of my bag, before dashing out the door as sneering jibes and taunts followed my footsteps. I struggled to hold back the tears, but managed to keep them at bay until I got home, locking the door behind me and falling face-down onto my bed.

I wallowed for a while until the sound of my phone beeping roused me. I tugged it from my pocket and saw several texts from Jamie.

Good luck with today, you'll be great!

Hey, I just saw you race back inside, are you okay?

Jane, I'm worried, I'm coming up to check on you.

I'm here. Please open your door?

I heard knocking, but couldn't face anyone, not while my failure and humiliation were still so recent. I sent him back a message of my own.

Not right now, Jamie. I'll come find you in a little while. I just need to be alone right now.

A moment later the knocking ceased, and I slumped back onto my bed. My phone pinged an email notification, and I opened it, my eyes welling with tears as I read the missive.

PC Jane Chérir,
We have received complaints against you from personnel and colleagues at the Metropolitan Police. We will be investigating allegations of conduct unbecoming a member of the constabulary. Until further notice, you are suspended without pay. Should these allegations prove correct, your employment with the Metropolitan Police Service will be terminated with prejudice. However, should

you resign under your own recognisance, we will close our investigations with a recommendation that you find other, more suitable employment in the future.
Yours,

So that was it. Another career down the drain and only minutes after I'd begun. What was it about me? I was perfect on paper, but once I was there in the flesh it all fell apart. Since I didn't want to drag things out, I sat down and wrote my letter of resignation, waving goodbye to another career. Today needed wine, copious amounts of wine, and it couldn't end soon enough.

∞∞∞

"Jane, sweetie-pie, chin up! So you've struck out twice, it's not the end of the world. I know you want to do things a little different than usual, to concentrate on creating connections, but if you're not careful, you'll burn out. We need to integrate fully before we can expect to do good work, the Ministry doesn't demand we start matchmaking straight off the bat. That's why they give us this probationary period, to ensure we'll be able to stick out our tenure."

I flopped back onto my couch, grumbling with annoyance down the phone. Yes, I knew I had time. Our only expectations were to find a job, settle into our home, and slide into human society without making any ripples. But I had hoped that I could get a head start on it all. After all, wasn't I smart? Didn't my degrees mean anything?

"I know, Luce, I know. Maybe working in such a public space wasn't right for me. Fingers crossed the Ministry can spin some magic and get my next option lined up without any further hassle."

"How's that delicious neighbour of yours?"

I chuckled.

"He's quite sweet. He was worried about me, saw me come home early. I've managed to brush him off for the moment, but I'm sure he'll be knocking on my door any minute to convince me to have a coffee and divulge all my sorrows."

Right on cue, a knock at my door proved my prediction correct. I quickly ended my call with Lucille and went to answer the door.

∞ ∞ ∞

Jamie

I was worried. I'd spotted Jane almost running back in this morning, and she'd been fobbing off my texts for the past several hours. I had to admit I'd been surprised at such a drastic career change and how she'd been able to join the Metropolitan Police so quickly. She'd brushed it off, saying "It's okay Jamie,

I studied nursing at uni and have worked as one previously. I only took those jobs while I waited for my application to join the MPS to be approved." Something felt a little off with her explanation, but who was I to argue?

Jane opened her door with her usual smile on her face, no sign of the distress from earlier.

"Everything okay with you Jane? What happened this morning?"

"Oh, everything's fine. Just a screw-up with the paperwork. The position I was supposed to take had already been filled, and there's not a spot for me. It's a shame really, I was looking forward to it. Oh well, I guess I'll have to just find something else."

Strange. She'd looked so devastated this morning, but then again, maybe it was just the disappointment? I dunno, I've got no clue when it comes to women.

"So, what's next then?"

She stood to one side and swept her hand to invite me inside.

"How does a bottle of wine and some cheese sound?"

Bloody brilliant, that's how.

Chapter Five

If I'd thought summer in England was grey and miserable, it had nothing on autumn's weather. Cold, wet, and windy. The delight of watching the leaves change colour soon dimmed after I'd had to pull yet another one off my face from where the last gust had splatted it. I was bundled up in a lovely warm knee-length pea coat, and a pair of knighted point calf boots encased my lower legs and kept them snug. My hair was tucked up inside a woollen slouchy beanie, and a matching infinity scarf kept my neck warm.

After my last disaster, I'd considered my options. Perhaps such publicly visible positions hadn't been the best choice, after all. As often as I'd studied the multitude of programmes in the Hub, perhaps I'd missed particular social cues. I'd noticed Jamie giving me strange looks from time to time, but since he'd never said anything, neither had I. My current choice of employment was more distant from the public eye, but still allowed me to work on creating and nurturing budding connections.

The school wasn't an overly large one, but that suited me fine. After all, wasn't it better to establish a rapport within a smaller community, build those relationships, and work my way up from there? I walked inside. The older building didn't retain heat that well, so I kept my coat, hat, and scarf on. I was sure once I found my room and cranked the heat up, it would be fine.

"Ms. Chérir, it's a pleasure! I'm Mrs Peterson. Shall I give you the grand tour?"

An older woman walked toward me, hand held out in greeting. This must be the headmistress. I shook her hand, a wide smile across my face.

"Yes please, I can't wait to get started!"

∞∞∞

I was buzzed. So far I'd taught two classes, both of them English. I'd heard nightmare stories about all-boys boarding schools, but my students had all been attentive and eager to participate. I was reaching for my pea coat when the headmistress walked into my room, the pleasant demeanour from this morning absent. Instead, hostility and disgust radiated from her in its place.

"I didn't think it possible, that someone with your credentials and training would be so foolish, so crass, so insulting, but I see I was wrong."

Wait, what? My confusion must've been evident on my face, because she scoffed at me.

"Oh, don't pretend butter wouldn't melt in your mouth! Your behaviour, your attitude, and the methods you employ to teach impressionable young minds are disrespectful, irresponsible, and highly unethical! I'll be reporting you to the school board, as well as the department. I'll have your file flagged with the DBS, and you'll never work with children again! Not if I have any say!"

I didn't understand. Both classes had been well behaved, and we'd gone through quite a lot of the set curriculum. What was she talking about?

"Pack up your things missy and leave the grounds before I call the police. You disgust me!" Mrs Peterson turned on her heel and marched out the door, waiting for me in the corridor. Impotent fury burned through my veins, but there was little I could do. I shrugged on my coat, buttoning it against the frigid building and its personnel, tucked my hair into my beanie, and looped my scarf over my neck. I held my head up proudly as I walked out the door, because no matter what falsehoods this woman spat at me, I knew I'd done a fantastic job teaching today. It was her loss.

∞∞∞

By the time I marched through the foyer of the Whitestar Apartments, I was steaming. I'd treated every person with respect and dignity, made sure I didn't use language that could be construed as crass or offensive, and taught beyond what had been set out for me with my two classes. Yet I'd been turfed out on my ear because the headmistress, along with other unknown colleagues, had deemed me as unprofessional, and not up to snuff with their expectations. Lucille was right, these people were jealous of my intelligence and skills, and wanted me out of the way so I wouldn't show them up.

I'd stopped off on the way home and bought a rotisserie chicken and some pre-packaged salads, as well as a bottle of wine. As I stood silently in the lift as it took me up to my floor, I sent Jamie a message.

Fancy joining me for dinner? Nothing special, just a chicken and salad.

His response was swift.

I'd love to. Want to bring it here though? I have three hungry mouths begging to be fed, and they love chicken!

I laughed. Three hungry mouths indeed. Walking to my door, I unlocked it and went inside, quickly changed into more casual clothing before I headed back to Jamie's door, food and wine in hand. He had it unlocked and open before I finished knocking, ushering me in while gently pushing his furry companions aside with one bare foot. Laughter bubbled out of me when he winced and swore, a feisty Mog attached to his ankle with teeth and claws.

"So, are you going to tell me how the little buggers behaved for you? Did any of them leave a thumb-tack on your chair? Any spit-balls ping you in the head?"

I curled my lip in irritation before smoothing my face.

"The students were fine, it was the staff that gave me problems. I don't need that kind of negativity in my life. Good riddance to bad rubbish!"

∞ ∞ ∞

Jamie

Wait, what? She's out another job? I watched as Jane cooed over the cats before heading toward my kitchen, unaware of my gaze. There was something strange going on with her, and I needed to find out what.

Chapter Six

I didn't know how they managed it, but the Ministry had pulled some strings and created a job opening for me one last time. If this one fell through, I'd be on my own, and have to comb through the human job sites to find work. They'd provide the necessary documentation, but nothing more.

The air was frigid, the sky a gunmetal grey. There had been the occasional snowflake or two, but it hadn't been cold enough to settle or stick. There had been several resident parties over the holiday break, and I'd adored the gift Jamie had shyly handed me; a pair of fluffy earmuffs with tiny leather cat ears perched on top of each cushion. I wore them now, bundled up against the cold in my pea coat and calf boots as I dodged fellow pedestrians. The lights and decorations had been pulled down from the street lights and store fronts, and as I walked past the statue of a long-dead monarch and into the red-brick building, red and pink garlands, hearts, and golden arrows dangled from the ceiling. Valentine's Day was still a month away, but that didn't matter to me. I loved Valentine's Day, all succubi and incubi did. After all, we often played the role of Cupid, it was one of our attributes. We always got a good chuckle over depictions of us—the only time we'd wear wings and a nappy was if we were playing around in that particular kink. Otherwise, we did our work unseen, stimulating interest, accentuating pheromones, and generally playing matchmaker. All of the top executives from the major dating sites and apps were succubi and incubi, their positions highly coveted.

I navigated my way to the help-desk and beamed at the duo seated there. One was a younger man, tall and slender, with dark hair and pale skin, the other was an older woman, her short silver hair styled back from her face, her eyes sharp yet friendly.

"Hello, how may we help you today?"

I glanced down to the woman's name tag and smiled, extending my hand.

"Hello Carol, I'm Jane Chérir, your new library assistant."

A beatific smile crossed her face, and she eagerly accepted my hand, shaking it warmly in hers.

"Oh, how wonderful! Welcome, welcome! This is Mark." She gestured toward the pale young man. "We were both excited to hear you'd be joining us! Come, let me show you around, and then we can get you settled in. We have several clubs and reading groups in today, would you mind supervising them at all? They'll give you a good feel for some of our regular visitors, and it should be a fairly easy start for you."

I beamed. It sounded perfect, and I said just that.

"Sounds perfect! What will I be doing besides

supervising?"

Carol rattled off my roles and responsibilities within the library as we strolled around the space, pointing out the different collections and sections for our patrons' use, as well as the café and toilets, before taking me back to the small staff room tucked away at the rear of the building.

"I'll leave you to it. There's a lockable cupboard over here for you to keep your personal items while working, and there's a space in the fridge for your lunch, if you bring it. Tea, coffee, milk, sugar and the like are all communal, we just ask you put in a couple of pounds every week toward costs. Otherwise, unless you've got any questions, I'll need to head back out."

I shook my head, and Carol left me to my own devices. I put my sandwich wrap in the fridge, shrugged off my coat and placed it and my purse in the cupboard, then locked it before snapping the key-chain onto my library lanyard. I headed toward the children's library where the mothers and babies reader group would soon arrive, almost giddy with excitement.

∞∞∞

I strolled back to the staff room, going over today's schedule in my head. There would be an influx of school students arriving soon, to take advantage of the number of homework help clubs the library offered. Not noticing the body blocking the doorway until I almost walked into them, I stumbled to a halt. My eyes fell on a rather angry looking gentlemen, the skin on his face and balding head a fiery red, his eyes glaring at me in furious disdain.

"So, you're the hussy strutting around this place like a trollop trawling through Soho! No, I won't have it, we won't have it! Get your stuff and get out, girly! You're an embarrassment, and I won't have you sullying the reputation of this library!"

I stood there open-mouthed. What the in the ever-loving Hell was wrong with people here? What was it about me that had them hating me almost on sight? I glanced over to where Carol and Mark both sat, him with an uncomfortably embarrassed look on his face, hers tight with both disappointment and sadness.

"I'm sorry Jane, but there have been complaints. You seem like a lovely young lady, if a bit...misguided. I hope you sort things out and find somewhere more suited to your...proclivities."

Right. Whatever. Fuming, I shoved my way past the puffed up little man blocking the doorway, knelt down to retrieve my coat and purse from the cupboard, pulled my sandwich wrap from the fridge, and tossed my key and lanyard to the table.

"You know, I'm getting really sick and tired of people treating me like I've got leprosy or something, just because I'm a square peg they're trying to shove into a round hole. I'm intelligent, enthusiastic, and hard-working, yet nobody seems to be able to look beyond the surface and see that. Your loss. I'm done."

Buttoning my coat, I stormed back out of the staff room, the angry little man following my steps all the way to the outer doors.

"I don't want to see you back here, do you hear me? You should be ashamed of yourself, walking around here like that!"

I turned back to him, an angry snarl on my lips.

"You might want to be careful who you insult, little man. You don't know me, you don't know what I'm capable of. So I suggest if you ever want to be able to get your tiny prick up again, you'll fuck off and leave me alone!"

With that parting salvo I marched away, leaving him blustering in my wake.

∞∞∞

I'd arrived home, changed into a pair of fuzzy pyjamas, and curled up on my couch with a mug of hot chocolate in my hand and a comedy playing in the background. Maybe Lucille was right, and I should try starting out small, find a job where I wasn't in constant contact with the public, yet still had human interaction. There were plenty of jobs out there like that, and many where a degree was completely unnecessary. I'd start combing through the job sites tomorrow, and see what I could pick up.

∞ ∞ ∞

Jamie

She'd lost another job. Another one. It didn't make sense. Jane was intelligent, well-spoken, friendly, and personable. She'd made quite a few friends here at Whitestar since she'd moved in, was sweet and considerate, and never pushed any boundaries. She seemed unaware of her own beauty and allure. The few times we'd been out together and someone had hit on her, she'd brushed them off with a kind word and a smile rather than the bitchy sarcasm my old colleagues would spout.

I'd been looking into her since November when she lost her place at that boarding school. I'd even called in some help from an old school friend of mine, and the results we'd discovered had been surprising. Jane had doctorates in medicine, engineering, and education. She had other degrees in accounting, business studies, and computer science. How she'd managed to rack up such an impressive portfolio in such a short time meant she was either a con-artist, or a certified genius. I was leaning toward the latter.

There was something else there, though. Something...strange. Something...unreal. Something...inhuman. The allure was irresistible, just as she was, and I would gladly drown in the oceans of her mystique. I needed to find out more.

Chapter Seven

It had taken me close to a month to get all my ducks lined up and score this job. My background check had held up under scrutiny, and I was given security clearance to enter my new workplace. It was in a village south-east of Croydon, and I was lucky that it was close enough to the bus and train stations that I could walk on nicer days, or catch a cab if it wasn't. Today I went with a cab. My employers would be out of the house for most of the day, and I felt relieved at the thought. My previous experiences had taught me that, if left alone, I could do my job and do it well— it was only if you introduced another person into my workplace that everything fell apart.

The cab dropped me in front of a set of electric gates, and using the passcode I'd been given to gain entry, I walked toward the house. The driveway was lined with walnut and yew trees with a large detached garage to one side, but it soon opened up to display a stunning house with a Georgian facade, rolling back into a manicured lawn and landscape. I paused for a moment, breathing in the quiet, before I headed to the front door.

I was lucky. My employers were willing to provide all of my supplies for me, as the house was listed and part of the local conservation area. I removed my pea coat, changed my calf boots for more comfortable Mary-Janes, and got to it.

There was no shame in cleaning, it was honest work with visible results. I scrubbed and scoured, waxed and polished, mopped and vacuumed the morning away. I took a brief break for an early lunch, then moved upstairs to the bedrooms.

I heard the front door open and close, a set of heavy footfalls thudded quickly up the stairs, followed by ones at a more sedate pace. The door to the room I was in burst open, a young man—probably no more than 17 years old—laughing over his shoulder to whomever accompanied him. I paused my work making the king-sized bed and stood to attention, my hands clasped in front of me, shoulders back, spine straight.

"Okay Mum, okay, I'll apologise to the bloody maid for dirtying up her clean floors!"

The youth turned back to face me, surprise registering at my presence before shifting into a sly smirk.

"Happy Valentine's Day to me! Uh, Mum, you might wanna come check this out. I think the maid might've got her wires crossed on her duties here." He called out back over his shoulder, his smirk never wavering. The set of footsteps that had followed him up the stairs came closer, revealing a statuesque woman, wearing a pair of tailored cream slacks paired with a plain jumper underneath a tweed jacket. Pearls sat at her throat and in each ear, her greying hair styled into a sleek bun at the nape of her neck. Her eyes widened in shock at my appearance, then narrowed angrily.

"What is the meaning of this? Who are you? How did you get in here?"

I twisted my fingers together nervously, dread filling my stomach at her tone.

"My name is Jane, I'm your new maid. You must be Mrs Taylor." I stepped forward and held out my hand in greeting, but dropped it soon after, her sneer of disgust telling. This woman obviously didn't shake hands with the help, because who knew what they'd been touching beforehand.

"You? You're my new maid? No. No you're not. You're fired, that's what you are. How dare you come into my house and behave in such a manner! Did you expect you could waltz in here, seduce my son, or even my husband? No. No. Out. Get out."

Face burning with humiliation, I kept my chin up as I walked carefully down the stairs and over to where my coat, bag, and boots were stowed. I changed out of my Mary-Janes, tucked them into my bag, before I shoved my arms into my coat and shouldered my bag. I paused for a moment, visualising Mrs Taylor before sending a pulse of energy her way. I refused to be cowed, to yell or scream or slam the door, but I would not be spoken to that way simply because I was an employee. A spark of spite lit up inside me as I heard Mrs Taylor shriek in response to her son's "Ew, gross

Mum, you shouldn't wear white pants if you're on your period!", a grim smile on my lips as I left the house, closing the door quietly behind me.

∞∞∞

I didn't remember much about my journey home. I was tired, so very tired. Today was supposed to be a fresh start, shiny and wonderful and full of opportunity. Instead, it was yet another failure stacked on top of a mountain of others. I ignored the happy couples cuddled next to each other on the train, glared at the love-hearts and flowers bedecking the store fronts encouraging people to spoil their significant other on this annual holiday of love, and snorted at Liz's cheery "Hello there Jane, happy Valentine's Day!" on my way to the lift. Was there a version of 'Bah, Humbug!' I could use for this day? I was alone, lonely, miserable, and a failure, so what was there to celebrate?

"Jane! Happy Valentine's Day! Want to join me for a coffee?"

I sighed and banged my head against my door. Jamie, dear, sweet Jamie stood in his doorway, a welcoming smile on his face. I looked over to him, unbuttoning my coat as I mulled it over. Maybe he could give me some advice, because I was all out of ideas.

"Come on in Jamie, we'll have it here. A word of warning though, I'm not in much of a mood to socialise."

I swung open my door and headed to the closet to hang my coat. The sound of the door closing almost disguised the muffled gasp from behind me, and I turned to see Jamie's flushed face, his eyes glued to the hem of my skirt where the lacy edge of my garter peeked out. I toed my boots off and kicked them into the closet before I padded barefoot through to my living area. I felt Jamie's eyes on my legs, tracing the black line of my back seam stockings, then back up to where the white satin apron ribbon was tied in a bow, stark in comparison to the black taffeta of my uniform. I pulled the lacy white cap from my head and tossed it onto the counter, removed the black velvet and white lace choker from my throat, and slumped onto my couch, the frills of my petticoats frothing around my thighs.

"What...what are you wearing?" Jamie's voice sounded strained, and the delicious scent of arousal wafted from him. I frowned, looking down at my uniform, and shrugged.

"I'm wearing my uniform. Today was my first—and apparently last—day working as a maid."

"Is...did...are...is that what you wore?"

I frowned again.

"Yes, I wore this. This is my maid's uniform. What else would I wear?"

Jamie made a choking noise, and I stood

quickly, concerned that perhaps something was wrong with him. He waved me back, a snort of laughter erupting from him as he bent double. After a moment or two he straightened and nodded to himself, muttering "Well, that would explain it all then," under his breath. I still heard him though.

"What would explain it all, Jamie? Do you have a reason as to why I've been fired from every single job I've held?"

He wiped a hand down his face then gestured toward me.

"Is that the type of thing you wore to each job?"

I nodded, and beckoned him to follow me. I walked into my bedroom and flung open the wardrobe door, each of my uniforms neatly hanging to one side. My beautiful nurse's uniform, pristine white with a red cross over the breast, cut to sit high and tight on my thighs, its deep v-neck plunging to mid-sternum. A matching white nurse's cap and white back seam stockings sat on the shelf below, along with a pair of white lace garters threaded with red ribbons.

Next was my police uniform, the filmy white blouse tailored to contour my body, the cravat perfectly situated under the plunging neckline to nestle between my breasts. The fitted black pencil skirt hit mid-thigh, with a high slit at the back to allow me to move freely. A wide black belt lay next to my PC cap, along with a pair of black fishnets paired with a set of black and white checked garters.

My teacher's attire followed, the pleated plaid

mini-skirt paired with an under-bust waistcoat in matching fabric, the gauzy white under-blouse almost identical to the sheer white stockings folded under of a set of plaid garters.

Last was my librarian garb, the tan coloured suede mini-skirt split high on each thigh, a diaphanous cream and tan pinstriped shirt with a black tie dangling from where the top button would sit in my cleavage. Stockings matching the colour and pattern of the shirt lay next to a thin black belt, a set of black garters, and a pair of round tortoiseshell glasses.

"Oh my god...you wore those to your jobs? No wonder you were fired!"

I spun around to glare at where Jamie stood, an exasperated expression on his face.

"What's that supposed to mean? Those are the uniforms and outfits recommended to me for those positions!"

"Who recommended them to you Jane? Tell me, who either hated you enough to sabotage each of your career choices, or was clueless enough to think them appropriate?"

I snapped my mouth shut. Nobody was supposed to know I wasn't human, that I wasn't from Earth. Jamie's eyes narrowed, a calculating look in them.

"Tell me something else, Jane. Where are you really from?"

My mind raced with panic as I desperately tried to remember my backstory. Nobody had really asked apart from Jamie, and in that moment I couldn't remember the exact details I'd given him.

"Um, I'm from, uh...um..."

"You're not from here, are you. You aren't even human, am I right?"

I was stunned. Shocked. Flabbergasted. Flummoxed. How? How would Jamie know this?

"Yeah, you aren't human. You gave yourself away, you know? Little things you did and said, the way people behave around you, even how you interact with animals. Things you should've known, but didn't, and other stuff you shouldn't have known, but did. I've been researching what you could be, and the only beings I could find that matched up with you is an angel, Cupid, or a succubus. So, which is it?"

I slumped to my bed, drained. I'd been discovered. Although it wasn't forbidden for select humans to know about us, the Ministry preferred those humans to be fully vetted beforehand, and somehow bound to us. We did our best to hide our true natures from humanity, but despite my best efforts, I'd been discovered.

"Succubus. I'm a succubus. We're often confused with Cupid, because part of our purpose is to create and nurture loving relationships. Today's supposed to be the highlight of our year, but mine? My Valentine's sucks! I'm a failure! I can't keep a job, haven't created or nurtured any relationships, and I've had enough. I'm going to go back to Hell once my probation is up!"

"Wait, what, you're leaving? No!"

I looked up just as Jamie strode over, a heated growl breaking from his throat as his lips descended onto mine.

∞∞∞

Jamie

God, she tasted sweet, so sweet, so perfect. I'd been aching to touch her like this for months, since that very first day we met. Her mouth opened under mine, her tongue snaking out to meet mine. Her arms looped around my neck, hands buried in my hair. I pulled her closer, tugging her body into mine and then held her there, pressed so tightly to me that not even a mote of dust would fit between us. It wasn't until Jane pulled back, overbalancing me so we fell to her bed, that my mouth broke away from hers.

"Jamie, what...why?"

"Why what?"

She ducked her head, avoiding my eyes. Feeling a bit guilty over the way I'd kissed her without her permission I loosened my grip and moved back a little, giving her some space.

"Why did you kiss me?"

I snorted back a laugh. How could she be so oblivious?

"Jane, I don't know if you've realised this or not,

but I've had the hots for you since the moment we met. You say you're a failure, that you haven't created or nurtured any relationships. What about this one? What about our relationship? You're my friend, you have been since day one. You check up on me when I've been working too hard, you go out to places with me, you talk and listen to me. You've created a solid foundation with me, and you've nurtured it to the point where I want more. I want to take the next step with you, and move beyond simple friendship."

Jane looked up at me, incredulity painted across her face.

"I...you....we....huh?"

I smiled indulgently down at her, tapped my finger against the tip of her nose, then pulled myself up and away.

"How's about you get changed out of your sexy French maid outfit there, and I take you out for dinner. We can talk it all over. Your options, your future, and the possibility of us becoming more."

I waited a beat, before asking the question that had sat on the tip of my tongue for weeks now.

"Jane Chérir, will you be my Valentine?"

Chapter Eight

Jamie had given me an hour to shower and get ready while he went home to do the same and feed his cats. By the time he knocked on my door, I was dressed in fleece-lined leggings, my boots snug around my calves, with an oversized chunky knit cardigan buttoned over a long-sleeved tee. My hair was up in a messy bun, and I had applied a light coat of make up to my face. I opened my door, a smile on my mouth as I took in Jamie. He was wearing dark grey skinny jeans that not only hugged his thighs and arse, but lovingly cupped the decent bulge at his front. His feet were shod in a pair of brown derby shoes, the colour matching his v-neck cable-knit jumper, a white tee peeking out at his throat. Offering me his arm, he escorted me to the lift and then out the foyer doors.

∞ ∞ ∞

Jamie took me to one of the nearby pubs known for its extensive cocktail and food menus. When he gave his name at the reservations desk, I lifted a brow, laughing as a blush covered his cheeks.

"I was hoping to ask you out, even if it was as friends."

I hugged his arm, a spear of excitement thrilling through me.

"I'm glad you thought ahead. Thank you in advance for tonight, no matter how it ends."

He pulled our clasped hands up to his mouth and pressed a soft kiss to my knuckles before tucking me under his arm as we followed the host to our table. We sat and made idle chatter while our waitress fetched our drinks, before glancing over the menu to place our orders. Once she'd left us alone, Jamie took one of my hands in his.

"So, tell me about where you're from, and what it's like there."

"I'm from Hell, or at least that's what humans call it. We're on a different plane of the cosmos, and deal with Earthly matters. Births, deaths, and all that exists between the two come under our jurisdiction. There are many different roles we take in guiding humans through their existence."

"What about after we die? Do we go and suffer eternal torment in lakes of fire to pay for our sins?"

I laughed. I laughed and laughed so much I had to wipe tears from my eyes.

"Oh, no, nothing like that. After you die, your soul goes to what humans call 'Heaven'. They deal with all things spiritual, including the rehabilitation and reincarnation of souls. There are those who choose to remain there, which is allowed, and others who join our ranks in Hell should they wish to take on a new role. Most people don't though, unless they had a solid connection to one of us during their human life."

"So, how do you go from living in Hell, to living on Earth?"

I paused momentarily at our waitress' approach, laden with our meals. Once she'd departed again, I continued my explanation between bites of succulent steak.

"There's an application process. You apply through the Ministry of Earthly Delights, and once approved, they provide you with enough start-up capital, resources, and accommodation for your probationary period. They'll help you find employment, but you have to do your due diligence beforehand and make sure you're up to scratch on any and all knowledge and expertise required. The Hub helps with this, and provides videos and footage of various real-life scenarios."

"The Hub? What's the Hub?"

"It's the Hub of all knowledge on humans. It used to be we only had written manuscripts and documents to rely on, but with the advent of television and then the internet, the Hub quickly became the font of all our knowledge. I don't know what we'd do without access to Porn Hub."

Jamie coughed, choking on a mouthful of food, but he waved me off when I made to go to him. Once he'd stopped coughing, he gulped down his drink, his eyes wide and incredulous.

"Did...did you just say Porn Hub?!"

I nodded, confused at his reaction.

"Yes, Porn Hub. Why, is there something wrong with that?"

"Something wro—. Yes, there's something wrong, something very wrong with basing your entire knowledge of the human world on a website dedicated to pornographic acts. Your Ministry fucked up big time in allowing it to continue. Jesus! No wonder you thought your 'uniforms' were appropriate workwear!"

My confusion turned to horror as Jamie spent the next half hour showing me what constituted an actual police uniform, medical scrubs, and appropriate attire for teachers and librarians. I was mortified to discover that, although it shared several attributes with what housekeepers and maids wore in their workplaces, most private cleaners weren't required to wear a uniform at all. Mine, although well made, was better off being kept aside for costume parties.

"Well, shit. I guess I'll have to notify the Ministry about their screw-up. I wonder why nobody has told them before?"

Jamie had ordered the Valentine's Day special for dessert, a platter for two with chocolate-lava cake, strawberries, marshmallows, churros, dipping chocolate, and whipped cream. Jamie fed me a bite of cake topped with cream, his eyes on my mouth as my tongue darted out to lick a stray droplet of chocolate from my lips.

He was holding back. I could feel the energy

thrumming through his veins, and could taste the tightly restrained desire with each breath. He'd been so considerate over dinner, not pressing the possibility of moving our relationship beyond friendship, but instead used our time together to help me, to alleviate my fears, and to set me on a better path forward.

I pulled on my powers a little, allowing my allure to pulse under my skin, and I smiled slowly as I watched Jamie's pupils dilate with desire.

"Jamie, you mentioned something earlier tonight, something about moving beyond friendship, into something more. Do you still want that, with me?"

"God yes!" Jamie blurted out, then stammered further, "I'd love to be more than friends with you Jane. I'd love it if we could date, maybe?"

"Jamie, do you want to be my boyfriend?"

"Fuck yes, I do. Jesus woman, what are you doing to me right now?"

I chuckled, the sound low and throaty, then stroked a finger down his arm.

"Well then, how about we get out of here and do something about that?"

Jamie's head whipped around, his arm raised to flag down our waitress as he called out, "Cheque please!"

∞∞∞

Jamie

I managed to hold things together until we stepped into the lift. It was empty, and as soon as the doors shut, I pressed Jane up against one wall, my hands cradling her face as my mouth devoured hers. I was hard, so fucking hard. I didn't know what was my natural reaction and what were her succubus abilities, but I didn't care so long as I'd get to bury my face, and then my cock, between those legs of hers.

The ding of our floor made me pull away, our breaths harsh and panting, and I couldn't tell who dragged whom to her door. It was the work of a minute for her to unlock and shove it open, and then we were back on each other, hands tugging frantically at clothing, feet kicking at shoes, lips melded together as we each tried to devour the other.

"My boots, they won't come off!" Jane complained as I reversed her into the bedroom. The backs of her knees hit the mattress and she fell, so I used the opportunity to tug her boots from her feet, tossing them behind me. She grinned up at me, hands at her waist before she moved them down, shimmying her way out of her leggings.

"Hey, I was gonna do that!" I protested half-heartedly, before pulling my jumper off over my head. I grinned as she responded, "Hey, I was gonna do that!", then tumbled down beside her, my hands already reaching for her. Our lips fused back together as I tugged the buttons of her cardigan open, my hand snaking up under her shirt to brush against her skin, warm and silky soft. Hers were delving under my shirt, the nails on her fingers scratching lightly down my spine. It felt good, so good, and I shuddered with pleasure. Jane tugged at my tee and I pulled away, giving her the space to pull it off me entirely. She paused, her eyes roaming over my body, and I saw the appreciation glowing in her eyes. I wasn't overly muscular, but I used the rooftop gym every day to keep in shape and I was glad I'd kept to my workout routine. I used her moment of stupefaction to remove her cardigan and tee, and groaned at the sight before me. Jane was beautiful. Long legs that rounded at the hips, nipping in some at the waist. She wasn't a stick, her curves were soft and lush, and her breasts were more than a handful—and I had large hands. She wore a matching lingerie set, sheer pink fabric doing nothing to hide her nipples or pussy, the cups and straps edged in pink lace, with red and pink hearts scattered across each piece.

I lightly traced my fingers down from her shoulder, over the swell of one breast, scratching lightly at the puckered nipple doing its best to poke through the bra. Down, down, over her ribs, circling her belly button, before following the line of her knickers across and over her hip. She lifted her leg and my hand cupped her arse cheek, her bare arse cheek. Fuck me, she was wearing French knickers. My cock surged painfully against the fly of my jeans, and a strangled groan escaped from my throat.

"Do you like, Jamie? Would you like to see

something even more special?"

I couldn't speak. My tongue had glued itself to the roof of my mouth, so I nodded. My eyes almost bugged out of my head when Jane lifted her other leg then parted them, exposing the slit in the crotch of her knickers. Not only was she wearing French knickers, they were crotchless. I'd died and gone to fucking heaven!

My mouth dove down onto hers, my desire and desperation to be inside her intense, but I didn't want things to end too quickly. My fingers traced over her body, following each dip and swell, lightly pinching at her nipples, and she squirmed underneath me, her own hands busy roaming my body.

"Jamie, fuck, Jamie, we need to get you out of these." Jane groaned as she fumbled with my fly, finally unsnapping the button at the waist. My rigid cock pushed against the zipper so hard that the moment she tugged, it slid down of its own accord. The relief in pressure felt so good I almost came in my boxers, but somehow managed not to. I stood, pulling both my jeans and boxers down my legs, the stiff length of my cock bouncing up and hitting my abs once released from its confinement. I stared down at where Jane lay on her bed, legs parted, her exposed pussy bare except for a strip of hair at the top. Her fingers played in the wetness there, and I fell to my knees like a devotee at the alter. My mouth watered, and I couldn't hold back any longer. I lunged, nuzzling my face between Jane's thighs, and buried my tongue inside her.

∞ ∞ ∞

Jane

Oh, fuck me, Jamie sure as Hell knew what to do with his tongue! I hadn't used any of my abilities since we'd left the pub, not wanting to influence our first time together that way. My hips jerked as his tongue travelled up to my clit, flicking over it rapidly before slowing to circle it. Flick, flick, circle. Flick, flick, circle. Flick, flick, circle. He kept doing that, each flick and circle setting my nerves alight, ramping up my pleasure, winding my body tighter than a spring. I was almost there, almost at the very precipice, when I felt a single finger trace around my opening, and it was enough to tip me over. My back arched, my body trembled, and my pussy spasmed around the finger he plunged inside me, gripping and milking it as each wave flooded over me. I was delirious with ecstasy, and felt a gnawing hunger deep in my belly, a pit of unfulfilled lust and desire, and I cried out as I lifted my hips.

"Up, off! I need them off! Please!"

Jamie must've understood my garbled demands, as he deftly pulled my saturated knickers down my legs, then reached behind me to unhook my bra. Moments later I was as naked as him, and I writhed and keened with the need to have him above me, inside me, joining with me as we scaled the heights of our desires. A crinkling noise sounded just before he knelt back on the bed, his knees between mine, his cock, so hard and eager, sheathed in a condom.

"Now, Jane?" He asked as he bent over to nibble softly at my nipples.

"Now, Jamie!" I demanded, impatient and greedy for him.

He took his cock in hand, stroked it once, before positioning it at my dripping slit. That first thrust, smooth and perfect, hit all the right places and had me clenching down hard around him. He was long and thick, filling me completely, stretching my pussy around his girth, the burn of his entry the perfect amount of pain to set me off once more. My pussy clamped down, rippling and milking his cock for all it was worth, and explosions of rapturous bliss permeated my entire being. I dimly heard Jamie cry out, "Fuck, fuck, I can't hold back, fuck!", and then his hands gripped my hips tight as his jerked and then stilled, his head thrown back as shudders wracked his body. Heaving for breath, he collapsed onto his elbows, eyes closed as he pressed his forehead to mine. I pressed a chaste kiss to his lips, and his eyes fluttered open, joy and adoration shining from their mossy depths.

"Happy Valentine's Day, Jane."

"Happy Valentine's Day, Jamie."

Carefully disengaging our bodies, Jamie went

to dispose of the full condom, and came back with a cloth, wet with warm water, and gently cleaned between my legs. After tending to us both he returned to my bed, wrapped his arms around me, and held me as we drifted and dozed the evening away.

∞ ∞ ∞

We were back at Jamie's place, after he'd made a pertinent point—he had cats that needed to be fed and coddled, and his bed was just as large as mine. We'd fed and petted the trio, and had curled up on his couch to talk things through. For now, we'd remain neighbours, although it would be a rare night we wouldn't be together. I was trying to puzzle out my job prospects, when Jamie turned to me, a mischievous grin on his face.

"Tell me, Jane, have you heard of Only Fans?"

Epilogue

The late-summer breeze was a welcome relief to the oppressive humidity. It had rained earlier, and I was on one of the roof terrace recliners, enjoying the bright sunshine after so much grey. A shadow fell over my face, blocking my sun, and I opened my eyes, shielding them with my hand. Jamie's happy face beamed down at me and I felt full to bursting, the love we felt for each other nourishing my succubi needs, constantly topping up my hunger.

"Hello there handsome, can I help you?"

Jamie chuckled and bent to press a heated kiss to my lips, a moue of disappointment forming on my mouth when he pulled away all too soon.

"Hello there beautiful, I have news!"

I sat up at that. Jamie and I had been inseparable since Valentine's Day, never spending more than a few hours away from each other. It had got to the point where I had practically moved in with him, so we'd applied for one of the three bedroom apartments in the building. Although it meant we'd have to break our current lease, the company was only too happy to accommodate us, seeing how we'd be staying with them. Unfortunately though, there hadn't been any units available, so we'd been put on a waiting list.

"Is there a unit? Did we get a unit?"

Jamie's grin only grew wider.

"We got a unit! And even better, it's on the 32nd floor, same as Cheryl and Rod! We'll be in number five!"

I chuckled. Even though the number wasn't thought as evil, it was 23 in reverse, and added up to the number five just as easily.

"The place will be available next month and comes unfurnished. We'll have to buy everything, but I think we can manage that between us, don't you?"

Jamie winked down at me, and I laughed. After all the pitfalls of my job-seeking, his suggestion our first night together had been right on the mark. I'd used each and every outfit from my failed jobs, and had created an Only Fans channel, playing out fantasies for a price. I'd even expanded my repertoire, adding a cheerleader, an angel, and a pirate-wench. My very first month I'd hit the top five in earnings, and since then I'd held the number one spot for the highest paid Only Fans account in the UK, and sat firmly in the top ten world wide.

The platinum and diamond engagement ring perched on my finger winked in the sun. Jamie had proposed to me the day before my probation period had ended, and I had accepted. I loved him more and more each day, and had contacted the Ministry of Earthly Delights immediately after to inform them of my change in relationship status. My assignment had been extended too, and once it was Jamie's time, we'd travel back to Hell together, and he'd become an incubus. Life was good, and it was only going to get better from here.

Acknowledgements:

First and foremost, I'd like to thank you, the reader, for taking a chance on this short story. I hope you found it as entertaining to read as I did to write. If you did like it, I'd *love* it if you could leave a review and rating on both Amazon and Goodreads. Reviews are the lifeblood for baby and indie authors like me. Thank you.

Next I'd like to thank R. Knight, a fellow indie author and Babe, for your willingness to read through and point out my errors or inconsistencies. You rock chickie!

To Becky Hodges, my Goddess of a PA. These first two months of 2022 have been rough on both of us. But through everything we've endured, you've been there, giving advice, cheering us on, and giving us your all. You're freaking awesome!

To my fellow Babes, thank you for being there. You are all my Golden Girls. Thank you for being my friends.

∞ ∞ ∞

And lastly, to my long-suffering hubby. Who needs Porn Hub when I've got you?

About the Author:

M.F. Moody writes Contemporary, Fantasy, and Paranormal Romance novels. She has a vivid and active imagination, and has used writing as an outlet during some very tumultuous times in her lifetime. She is often blunt to the point of brutality, has a dark and warped sense of humour, has absolutely no filter, and aspires to the giddy heights of the gutter. She is also a survivor of domestic abuse, depression, and anxiety, and tries to use her experiences to become a better person, as well as help others.

M.F. Moody is married to a VERY understanding man, and together they have a boy-child, 3 cats, and apparently WAAAAY too many books and alcohol, especially as she's the only one who drinks. Although really, is there such a thing as having too many books? And as for the alcohol, well, she's Australian. They live in a little corner of Kent in the UK, and she enjoys confusing the locals with her accent and colloquialisms, reading, coffee, wine, reading, baking, sleeping, and did we mention reading?

You can find M.F. Moody below:
Website: M.F. Moody Books
Facebook: M.F. Moody Author
Facebook Group: The Temperamental Bookwyrms
Amazon
Discord: The Stable of Smut
Instagram
TikTok
Spotify

Printed in Great Britain
by Amazon